The Not-So-Faraway
Adventure

Inspired by Gerry Arbeid, an extraordinary Zaida — A.L.

For my family, with love … And a special thanks to Yvette Ghione and
Marie Bartholomew for their patience, hard work and expertise — I.L.

The Italian pastries mentioned in the story, *zeppole* (TSEHP-poh-leh), are
deep-fried dough balls usually sprinkled with sugar. Sometimes they also
have custard, jelly, pastry cream or other delicious fillings.

Text © 2016 Andrew Larsen
Illustrations © 2016 Irene Luxbacher

Kids Can Press acknowledges the financial support of the Government of
Ontario, through the Ontario Media Development Corporation's Ontario
Book Initiative; the Ontario Arts Council; the Canada Council for the Arts;
and the Government of Canada, through the CBF, for our publishing activity.

Published in Canada by
Kids Can Press Ltd.
25 Dockside Drive
Toronto, ON M5A 0B5

Published in the U.S. by
Kids Can Press Ltd.
2250 Military Road
Tonawanda, NY 14150

www.kidscanpress.com

The artwork in this book was rendered in Photoshop.
The text is set in Goudy Old Style.

Edited by Yvette Ghione
Designed by Marie Bartholomew

This book is smyth sewn casebound.
Manufactured in Shenzhen, China, in 10/2015 by Imago

CM 16 0 9 8 7 6 5 4 3 2 1

Library and Archives Canada Cataloguing in Publication

Larsen, Andrew, 1960–, author
        The not-so-faraway adventure / written by Andrew Larsen ;
illustrated by Irene Luxbacher.

ISBN 978-1-77138-097-3 (bound)

I. Luxbacher, Irene, 1970–, illustrator II. Title.

PS8623.A77N68 2016   jC813'.6   C2015-903264-4

Kids Can Press is a *Corus*™ Entertainment company

The Not-So-Faraway Adventure

Andrew Larsen • Irene Luxbacher

Kids Can Press

Theo's Poppa was an explorer.
He had been everywhere.
He kept an old trunk packed with the pictures, postcards, maps and menus that he had collected on his adventures. Whenever Theo looked inside the trunk, she found something interesting.

There was Poppa with Nana in front of the Eiffel Tower.

There he was sitting on a scooter. He looked so different when he was young!

There was a menu from the Italian restaurant where he discovered *zeppole*.

And look at that map of New York City! It had an X marked on it. Theo wondered what it meant. Maybe it was another one of Poppa's discoveries.

Someday Theo wanted to be an explorer, too.

Just like Poppa.

It was almost Poppa's birthday.
Theo was trying to think of the perfect gift.
She thought of drawing Poppa a picture. But would
that be special? She drew him pictures all the time.
She thought of buying him a little something. But he
always told her he had everything he needed.

"What do you want to do for your birthday tomorrow, Poppa?" Theo asked.

"Nana and I always went out for a meal," he said after a good long think. "I remember, once, we drove for a whole day to get to a little restaurant on a beach by the ocean. We had the best clam chowder we had ever tasted."

"I have an idea!" said Theo.

"Hmm," said Poppa, still thinking about that day with Nana.

"I know a beach!" said Theo. "We can take the streetcar!"

"The streetcar?"

"I went to the beach on a streetcar with my class last year."

"I haven't been to the beach for a long time," said Poppa.

"There's even a restaurant," said Theo.

Poppa's eyes lit up.

It wasn't long before Theo and Poppa were sketching a map.

"This is where we are," said Poppa, marking an X on the page.

"And this is where the streetcar goes," said Theo, drawing a long line from where they were to where they wanted to go. "Here's the way from the streetcar to the beach." She made a dotted line, like footprints. "And the restaurant is right here!" She marked another X on the map.

"And there's you, and there's me," laughed Poppa, drawing two smiling faces. "We're happy because we've just discovered something delicious to eat."

"Are you ready for your birthday adventure, Poppa?" Theo asked the next day as they climbed onto the streetcar.

"You bet!" he said.

The signal bell clanged, and the streetcar lurched forward.

Poppa and Theo took their seats. They smiled at the feel of the rumble beneath their feet.

"I'm excited!" said Poppa, squeezing Theo's hand.

"Me, too, Poppa," said Theo, answering his squeeze with two of her own.

They sailed by bookstores, bakeries, restaurants and schools.
Theo waved to all the passing people.
Some waved back.

When they got close to their stop, Theo rang the bell.

She checked their map as they walked down the road that led to the park that led to the beach. Then she looked ahead, and …

The world opened up!
The beach stretched as far as she could see.
The blues of the sky washed into the blues of the water.
Theo felt like she was stepping into one of Poppa's postcards.

"I used to come here in the summer when I was a little boy," said Poppa. "I thought this was the ocean."
"Let's pretend it *is* the ocean, Poppa," said Theo.
"Let's pretend we're on a faraway adventure."

They took off their shoes and sank their feet into the cool of the sand.

They explored the shallow waters along the shore.

They found stones smooth enough for skipping and some that looked just like jewels.

Theo put a single stone in her bag for keeping.

"Can I use your camera, Poppa?" asked Theo.

"Of course," he said.

"Smile," said Theo.

Poppa smiled, and Theo took a picture of him and the beach and the water and the sky.

Theo and Poppa walked along the beach to the restaurant.
They sat on the patio.
They ordered gazpacho soup.
It was cold ...
It was tangy ...
It was terrific!
"That was the best gazpacho I've ever tasted," said
Poppa, loudly slurping the last of the soup from his spoon.
"And we discovered it together!" said Theo.
Poppa took a picture of Theo slurping her soup from
her spoon.
"I'm going to put this picture in the suitcase," he said.
"Really?" asked Theo.
"Really," said Poppa.

On their way back to Poppa's, they sailed by schools,
restaurants, bakeries and bookstores.
Theo waved to all the passing people.
Some waved back.

"Do you know what I like best about going on adventures?" asked Poppa, squeezing Theo's hand.

"What?" said Theo, squeezing back twice.

"Coming home."

When they got back to Poppa's, there was a surprise waiting for them.

Theo's mom and dad had decorated Poppa's apartment with balloons and streamers.

And there were cupcakes from Poppa's favorite bakery.

Theo put a candle in a cupcake with blue icing because it reminded her of their day at the beach.

"Happy birthday, Poppa!" she said. "Make a wish!"

"It already came true, Theodora," said Poppa. "You should make a wish."

So Theo made a wish and blew out the candle.

But before she had a taste of her cupcake, Theo went to Poppa's trunk.
She carefully folded the map and put it inside.
She took the stone from her bag and put that inside, too.
Then Theo went back to the party …

And ate the best cupcake she had ever tasted!